UNDER the FIG TREE

By Emily Reed

Copyright © 2004 by Emily Reed

All rights reserved. No part of this publication may be reproduced in any form or by any means, electronic or mechanical, including photocopy, recording, or any information storage and retrieval system, without permission, in writing, from the publisher.
All characters are fictional. Any resemblance to persons living or dead is coincidental and quite unintentional.

ISBN 0-9755739-7-7
First Printing 2004
Cover art and design by pinfeather
Chapter illustratioins by pinfeather
Book design by pinfeather and Emily Reed
Author's portrait by Emily Reed

Published by:
Dare 2 Dream Publishing
A Division of Limitless Corporation
Lexington, South Carolina 29073
Find us on the World Wide Web
http://www.limitlessd2d.net

Printed in the United States of America and the UK by

Lightning Source, Inc.

Acknowledgements

First and foremost, my heartfelt thanks to pinfeather for an outstanding editing job, for the wonderful illustrations and cover that grace this book, and, most important, for providing continuous inspiration. Thanks also to Lynn Johnson, whose help and advice were invaluable in editing key parts of the manuscript. I am grateful to the members of my online writers' group, whose supportive feedback helped make this book a reality. Special thanks to Sam and Anne, of Limitless Dare 2 Dream, who agreed to publish this effort.

To my friends who had unswerving faith in me, and insisted I should go ahead and do this despite my doubts and misgivings: I can never thank you enough for your support, and for the many, much needed, kicks in the posterior! You know who you are.

*To my lover,
My inspiration.*

Table of Contents

Chapter 1: *Dates* 2

What I Could Do	3	My Engineer in Teal	19
More!	4	Biases	20
You Are	5	Esperando	21
Affirmation	6	Decadence	22
Give and Take	7	Sublime	23
Come With Me	8	Goddess	24
I Have a Love	9	Overcome	25
The Laws of Nature	10	Adagio	26
Cavewoman's Claim	11	Teneramente	27
The Joys of C	12	Mesmerized	28
Convergence	13	Enigma	29
Magic	14	Will You	30
The Myriad You	15	I Remember	31
My Irish Lass	16	At Last	32
I'm No Linus	17	When?	33
Some Women	18	Let Them	34

Chapter 2: *Pomegranates* 36

Queimadura	37	Hot to Trot	47
The Naked Truth	38	On the Edge	49
The Best Laid Plans	39	Do You Know?	50
Victoria's Secret	40	Hunger	51
The Burning Bush	41	Halloween	52
Double H	42	Thankful	53
Reveille	43	Balance	55
40-30-30	44	Homage	56
Amen	45	Touch Me	58
Come To Me	46		

Chapter 3: *Vines* 60

Marathon!	61	Insomnia	69
The 27th Mile	62	Dr. J.	70
Again?!	63	Ode to a Speculum	71
A Poet	64	Femme I Am!	72
Sex in Iambic	65	Online Blues	74
Taking the Plunge	67	Reaper	76
You've got SPAM!	68		

Chapter 4: *Figs* 78

Forbidden Fruit	79	Hindsight	95
Demons	80	Wheels	96
Pyrite	81	Tick Tock	97
In Limbo	82	In Time	98
No Return	83	Scars	99
Out of Sorts	84	In Vain	100
The Midas Touch	85	Full Circle	101
Enough!	86	Revelation	102
Critical Point	87	Cheers	103
Cést La Vie	88	Faith	104
Choice	89	The Flip Side	105
Disillusionment	90	Dawn	106
Boyling	91	Hypnagogic	107
Shepherd	92	Missing You	108
Salva Me	93	Don't Give Up	109
Graveyard	94	Regrets	110

Chapter 5: *Olives* 112

Ashes to Ashes	113	Shaheed	118
Thieves	114	Milk and Honey	119
Punch Cards	115	Our Time	120
Another Day	116	Innocence	121
Roulette	117	Into Sleep	122

Chapter 6: *Wheat and Barley* 124

Party Girls	125
In Her Image	128

Chapter One

Dates
(Phoenix dactylifera)

What I Could Do

I could be a superstar
Drive a sleek, expensive car
Win a Golden Palm at Cannes
Sign my name for every fan

I could model for Chanel
Have the critics say *"quelle belle"*
Drip with jewelry and gold
Such a vision to behold

I could bring about world peace
Cause all poverty to cease
With Annan and Kim Dae Jung
Oslo in the afternoon

I could fly to outer space
Build a high-tech lunar base
Solve for superstrings by dawn
Find the fabled graviton

I could live my every dream
But I know that it would seem
Less than perfect, full of flaws
And I'd give it up, because

It would not mean a thing without you.

More!

More than man loves his youth
Or Socrates – truth
More than poets love rhyme
Or clocks – telling time
More than divas love fame
Or gamblers – the game
More than fire loves the air
Or Werther – despair
More than butter loves bread
Or needles – the thread
More than winter loves snow
Or arrows – the bow
More than all that I know
I love you so.

You Are

A glimmer of sunlight in overcast skies
A vision of beauty to disheartened eyes
A haven in which I can shed all disguise
Immutable truth in the midst of the lies.

A wellspring of strength burning steady and bright
The dawn that announces an end to the night
A refuge I seek from the heat of the fight
The answer to every equation I write.

An island of calm in the turbulent flow
Enveloping warmth when the icy winds blow
A shelter from harm when defenses are low
The love that sustains me wherever I go.

Affirmation

When your hand enfolds mine
As we walk down the street
When you look at me so
And my heart skips a beat
When the world fades away
As I'm wrapped in your kiss
When we make slow, sweet love
And we redefine bliss
When our bodies press close
As our passion burns bright
When I wake in your arms
And it simply feels right
When just being with you
Has me up on cloud nine
Then I know this is it:
I am yours, and you're mine.

Give and Take

In the taking, there is giving
There's complete and utter trust
Because what we have between us
Far surpasses simple lust.

Every kiss my mouth delivers
I can feel on my own skin
Every touch of mine upon you
I in turn feel deep within.

Every moan and every whimper
I can't help but echo back
That your pleasure fuels mine, love
Is a clear and certain fact.

In the giving, there is taking
There's a blurring of the line
And the love we share between us
So much more than words define.

Come With Me

Come with me on a journey new
An adventure undertaken
With love our guide to lead us true
Our former lives forsaken.
Look and see what my heart holds
In every chamber, you
With each hot pulse my love unfolds
And warms my body through.
Take my hand, I'll hold on tight
And never let you go
Don't question this, it feels so right
So let your feelings show.
Let me love and cherish you
With every breath I take
Do with me what lovers do
Exquisite love we'll make.
I can't explain how you became
An all-consuming need
But this I know: you feel the same
You too, this love will feed.

I Have a Love

I have a love more rich than gold
It keeps me warm when life is cold
From love's sweet cup I drink my fill
A tonic warding off the chill.

I have the world within my hand
A love as pure as pristine sand
A soothing warmth surrounding me
An ocean of tranquility.

I have a love that gives me life
Sustaining me in times of strife
A shield deflecting every blow
To carry with me where I go.

I have a love that makes me whole
A healing balm upon my soul
A love that's wondrous, deep and true
All this and more, I have in you.

The Laws of Nature

You're the current through my circuit
And together we will spark
You're the ground to my high voltage
And together we will arc.

You're the metal to my magnet
And together we attract
You're the mass to my momentum
And together we impact.

You're the bottom to my top quark
And together we're confined
You're the proton to my neutron
And together we're combined.

You're the helium to my neon
And together we will lase
You're the neutron to my fission
And together we will blaze.

It's in every law of physics
From the atoms to the stars
We were meant to be together
And the universe is ours.

Cavewoman's Claim

I want to mark you, love, as mine
I'll hang a flashing neon sign
Around your neck, and it will say
"I'm Em's, too late, so go away!"
Then everyone will surely know
Where they are not allowed to go
Because you're mine and I don't share
So trespassers had best beware
And all who see will envy me
Since by your side they cannot be
My claim on you I want to stake
And baby, please, make no mistake
These are no idle words I speak
I have a large possessive streak
Where you're concerned, I can't keep cool
Neanderthal emotions rule.

The Joys of C

Let me scanf your body, baby
#define your parameter space
Each floating point variable explored
With double precision embraced.
For each time I tell you I love you
I'll increment counter by one
Debugging all of your functions
Who knew C could be so much fun?
While our love isn't equal to null
This loop will continue to run
My file pointer's aimed straight at you
All external objects are shunned
Let me code your heart straight into mine
Printf the results out in bold
The value your function returns
This programmer wants more than gold.

Convergence

I hadn't been looking, was caught unaware
Just thought you were someone with whom I could share
A friendship and laughter, some good times together
I never expected love, like a pinfeather,
To peek out; so hesitant, scared to emerge
I didn't quite see I was right on the verge
Of love this consuming and wondrous and new
The orderly course of my life's cast askew
I'm tipped upside down and I'm turned inside out
By unforeseen feelings that leave me no doubt
I've finally found the lost piece of my heart
It's right there with you, and it was from the start.

Magic

I turn it over in my mind
It's something I cannot define
This magic that is you and me
Defies all rationality
A spell on me was surely cast
That kept me dormant these years past
Until you came and woke me up
Now I drink deeply from life's cup.
A fire's coursing through my veins
As finally I take the reins
Of my own life in my two hands
And heed none but my own demands.
The feelings sweeping through me, more
Than I have ever known before,
Consume me, as I am reborn
The veil from over my eyes torn.
No going back, nor would I try
My own true self I won't deny.
And you have done all this for me
Revealed how wondrous love can be
Your eyes, your touch, your words convey
Quite clearly to me every day
Beyond a shadow of a doubt
That this is what love's all about
And what we share, so clear and strong
It's magic; it cannot be wrong.

The Myriad You

You're the reason I still smile
Between the bouts of tears
You're the reason I still cope
Despite the crushing fears
You're the light that shines on me
And penetrates the dark
You're the color in a world
That otherwise is stark
You're the hope that burns in me
And banishes despair
You're the one who's heaven-sent
The answer to my prayer
You're the woman I adore
The only one for me
You're the one who'll wear my ring
My love, it's meant to be.

My Irish Lass

I have myself an Irish lass
She's mighty fine, and real high class
She's got a healthy dose of sass
And my, she's got a lovely ass!

To my good luck I'll raise a glass
On Guiness, though, I think I'll pass
There is no greener than my grass
I have myself an Irish lass!

I'm No Linus

You're my security blanket
Want to carry you around
But don't worry, I'm no Linus
I won't drag you on the ground.

Want to wrap you all around me
Tuck you underneath my clothes
Did I mention I'm commando?
I ain't got no need for "those"!

I think flannel must be jealous
Of the texture of your skin
Polar fleece is over-rated
Love, you warm me from within.

Some Women

Some women have wonderful figures
They're perfectly formed works of art
Some women have faces that trigger
Your hormones, and speed up your heart.

Some women have brains just like Einstein's
Their I.Q.s are way off the scale
Some women have clever and quick minds
That make other attributes pale.

Most women possess some of both, it's
A balance between brains and looks
But *my* sweetheart's perfect – both beauty *and* wits
And to top it off, she even cooks!

My Engineer in Teal

My gorgeous engineer in teal
Exudes a ton of sex appeal
The clothes she wears cannot conceal
Her form, in every way ideal!

There is no heart she cannot steal
No head she can't with ease make reel
No woman she cannot make keel
Right over, and at her feet kneel!

Her clothing I will slowly peel
Away, and every curve reveal
She makes a most delightful meal
Of which I will partake with zeal!

I love the way she makes me feel
So good, it sometimes seems surreal
It's very simple, here's the deal:
I love my engineer in teal!

Biases

So, you tell me I am biased in the way I look at you
You scoff at claims I lay to an objective point of view
Refusing to believe my protests that my words are true
Well, love, it's time you opened both your eyes, and got a clue!

But knowing how you cling to your opinions stubbornly
I don't expect that you'll just acquiesce submissively
To state my case beyond refute is what I need to do
So let me tell you what I see, love, when I look at you.

I see the friend who stood by me and wouldn't let me fall
When so melodramatically I thought I'd lost it all
I see a woman who is kind and thoughtful, even sweet
(Although I'm quite sure that's a word you'd like me to delete)
I see the woman who is there for me in every way
The one that somehow always knows exactly what to say
I see the woman who has shown me what love's all about
(The one who is responsible for all this mush I spout)
I see the woman I desire, whose touch ignites a blaze
Whose love for me is clear to see in her intense blue gaze
I see the woman that I love with everything I've got
The way you only read about in Harlequins, I thought
But now I know that it's no book, it's you and me, it's real
And best of all, I know I'm not alone in how I feel.

So, now I hope you see, I'm as objective as they come
You may as well be graceful as to logic you succumb
Convincing you anew will only take up precious time
That could be so much better spent, and that would be a crime!

Esperando

Through long and lonely hours when we're apart
When grief and sadness, vise-like, squeeze my heart
The loving words you write help ease the pain
And comfort me, until we meet again.

When memories of you are all that's left
When you have gone, and left my heart bereft
The loving words you speak help warm me through
Reminding me that we will meet anew.

Though hours may drag their feet as they go by
And rules of physics time seems to defy
Our wait *will* end, you'll be with me at last
And time for words of comfort will be past.

Your eyes, your lips, your touch will speak to me
All clearer than mere words could ever be
And as your loving touch pervades my soul
I'll know again the joy of being whole.

Decadence

A bottle of wine
Chilled to perfection

Honey-dipped strawberries
A tasty confection

An assortment of chocolates
Dark, bittersweet

Our bodies swaying
To passion's beat.

Sublime

Hey, you! I have to let you know
That I'm just aching for you so
I need your touch to rescue me
From fevered flights of fantasy
From dreams that leave me unfulfilled
No substitute for fingers skilled
I need to feel your lips on mine
To feel the tingling down my spine
That heralds better things to come
As to our loving we succumb
Your name the mantra on my lips
The tune to which I rock my hips
Your touch a need I can't deny
Far past the point of asking why
Your love the ballast for my soul
A gift sublime, it's made me whole.

Goddess

Let me worship at the altar
Of your body with my own
You, the font of a desire
Unlike anything I've known
You're the wellspring of a passion
That I cannot seem to slake
An unquenchable desire
Of your blessings to partake.
Let me delve into your secrets
Every mystery you hide
I'm your acolyte, devoted
And I will not be denied
Let me worship at your altar
And then touch me in return
Be my Goddess, be my lover
And together we will burn.

Overcome

As I was headed out, I paused
For just one more quick look
I saw her lying on the bed
And that was all it took.

Her head was pillowed on her hand
Her body stretched out, bare
I felt a tightness in my chest
A sudden lack of air.

I met her eyes, my mouth was dry
I felt my legs grow weak
A surge of feeling so intense
Too overcome to speak.

All thoughts of everything but her
Fled, lost without a trace
As I turned back toward the bed
And into her embrace.

Adagio

A pale patch of moonlight
Is painting your body
A shimmering, silvery hue
My eyes travel over
A live chiaroscuro
The breathtaking vision that's you.

From high, angled cheekbones
To full, sculpted lips
To a stubborn, delectable chin
My eyes linger over
The light and the shadows
That dapple your satiny skin.

As if in a trance
I cannot look away
From the wondrous tableau facing me
My eyes wander over
Your softly lit curves
As my body reacts, helplessly.

You shatter the spell
As you move toward the bed
I can feel your heat pressed against mine
My eyes are shut tight
As desire explodes
With a force I can't hope to define.

Familiar and comforting,
Under my ear
I can feel your heart calming its beat
My arms hold you tight
As our bodies entwine
And I know that with you I'm complete.

Teneramente

The crackling sounds of the fire
Are loud in the warm, quiet room
The smell of the burning pine logs
Mingles pleasantly with your perfume.

You're lying relaxed on the quilts
Bathed in flickering orange and red
The scent of massage oil wafts up
Playing sensual games with my head.

I smooth my hands over your back
Gently tracing the hollows and dips
The world with its cares and concerns
From my consciousness easily slips.

And as thoughts to emotions give way
Feelings rise in me, passionately
I cannot seem to find the right words
To encompass what you are to me.

The fire is fading to coals
But my love for you burns strong and bright
Intense, all-consuming and deep
There's no doubt in my mind. This is right.

The embers have faded to black
And contentment suffuses my soul
I marvel how lucky I am
In our love I am finally whole.

Mesmerized

Mesmerized
By the smoothest of skin
Where to begin
To express
What you are to me?

Tantalized
By each elegant curve
Words cannot serve
To define
Your effect on me.

Hypnotized
By the look in your eyes
Love undisguised
And I know
Only you for me.

Enigma

So many things about you I don't know
What shaped you into who you are today
What made you laugh in carefree happiness
What made you cry in heartfelt loneliness
What dreams you harbored as a little girl
What wishes you once made upon a star
Would you go back and change things if you could
Or are you happy now with who you are?

So many things about you I don't know
You keep your distance, holding me at bay
I wonder if you even realize
How wide the chasm sometimes seems from here.
I want to leap across and bridge the gap
I wish I could just walk into your heart
And breaking down the walls that block my way
Be welcomed there with open arms, to stay.

Will You?

Will you lend me your strength when I falter and doubt
Let me rest in your arms as I face the next bout?

Will you love me as is, imperfections and all
Regardless the reason, not letting me fall?

Will you give yourself over, surrender each part?
You can trust me to treasure the gift of your heart.

Will you bare heart and soul, and be left open wide?
Know that no matter what, I will stay by your side.

Will you lean on me sometimes, reach out for my hand?
It will always meet yours and together we'll stand.

Will you wear my ring proudly, and give yours to me
As we look to a future where our love is free?

I Remember

I remember the feel of your skin
Glistening so, in the candle-lit room
My hands eagerly tracing your curves
By desire I was wholly consumed.

I remember the taste that is you
Unlike anything I'd ever known
Drinking with an unquenchable thirst
Driven on by your increasing moans.

I remember the scent of our love
Slowly spreading, suffusing the room
Flowing through me with each breath I took
So much sweeter than any perfume.

I remember the sound of your heart
Beating steadily under my ear
As I pillowed my head on your chest
And the rest of the world disappeared.

I remember the look in your eyes
Full of love, all directed at me
Leaving no room for doubt in my mind
At your side's where I needed to be.

I remember, I cannot forget
How it felt to be finally whole
And until I am with you again
Know that you hold a part of my soul.

At Last

Clothing haphazardly on the floor strewn
Breath grows unsteady as hearts beat in tune
Hands, ever greedy, caress every part
Touch conveys more than mere words can impart.

Passions rise swiftly, abate, rise again
Too strong and sweeping to want to contain
No clock to time us and tear us apart
No obligations, save those of the heart.

No turning back for one last glimpse of you
One bed to share, and to sleep the night through
Wrapped in your arms, feeling sated and spent
Wrapped in your warmth, feeling safe and content.

When?

As the distance grows so great
And the pain does not abate
I can't help but wonder when
I will hold you close again.

And the vultures circle 'round
Hoping we will run aground
For their selfish reasons each
Wishing love beyond our reach.

Then I hear the words you said
Sounding strongly in my head
And my heart is fortified
Time *will* find us side by side.

Let Them

Let them gloat and let them think
We're coming to an end
Let them mouth their platitudes
And let them condescend.

You and I, we know the truth
It's etched upon our skin
The certainty that we'll prevail
Sustains us from within.

Chapter Two

Pomegranates
(Punica Granatum)

Queimadura

God, how you make me burn
Melting me with your kiss
Teasing me with your touch
Baby, I yearn for this
Arching into your hands
Wanting you deeper still
Feeling your tongue on me
Do with me what you will
Take me, I need to give
All that I am to you
Need you to understand
This love that I feel is true
Reaching the highest peak
Yours is the name I cry
Quieting in your arms
Sated, content, I lie
In between ragged breaths
Holding each other tight
Your words of love meet mine
Echoing through the night.

The Naked Truth

I love you when you're naked and in bed
I love you clothed as well, it should be said
I love you when you're naked in the shower
All wet and ready for me to devour
I love you when you're naked as you cook
You make me sizzle, love, with just a look
I love you when you're naked on the couch
The goosebumps on my arms to that can vouch
I love you when you're naked in my arms
At leisure I can then explore your charms
I love you any way you care to be
As long as it entails that you're with me.

The Best Laid Plans

Oh baby, you're so fine
I'm so happy that you're mine
Let's drink a little wine
And then on you I'll dine.

Your taste is so refined
And so finely honed, your mind
Your curves are well-defined
And baby, that behind!

You know you make me burn
How you make my insides churn
To take you, love, I yearn
I doubt you'll get a turn.

I don't think you'll complain
But instead in sweet refrain
Your voice will cry "again"
As for release you strain.

And when you reach that peak
You might feel the need to shriek
Your limbs will feel so weak
You won't have breath to speak.

I'll hold you to me tight
And reach out and dim the light
Then kiss you sweet good-night
Because love, we know it's right.

Victoria's (Not So) Secret

I gave my love a demi-bra
I had it shipped from Vic's
And with it came a matching thong
That looked nice in the pics.

The demi-bra was quite low cut
Revealing lovely curves
And luscious nipples peeking through
Were savory hors d'oeuvres!

The thong revealed more than it hid
(Exactly as I'd planned!)
That sexy ass accessible
To my caressing hand.

The things she did for that teal set
I'll never be the same
The models in those catalogs
She put them all to shame!

But one small thing I must confess
(I hope you will not scoff)
The part that I enjoyed the most
Was taking it right off!

The Burning Bush

I took my shoes from off my feet,
I took the rest off too
I stood before the burning bush
Prepared to worship you.

I knelt down on my knees in awe
I bent my head down low
I looked upon the burning bush
And felt the fire grow.

I put my hand inside the fire
I felt the scorching heat
I felt the flames engulfing me
With no thought of retreat.

I ventured then to taste the fire
I licked the tongues of flame
I worshipped at the burning bush
Not stopping 'til you came.

I saw the bush was not consumed
Although it burned with fire
It must indeed be holy ground
The font for my desire.

Double H

I have a pair of dyke-ish boots
I'm wearing them with pride
My stonewashed Levi 502's
Ride low on my backside
My bluish-purple navel ring
Was custom made for me
I keep it hidden from the world
For you alone to see
My satin Vic's peek from my jeans
Each time I stretch my arms
The better to beguile you and
Ensnare you with my charms
Alas, you are not here to see
This vision I describe
A trip to the Midwest at once
For you I must prescribe
And then these dyke-ish boots can go
The jeans can hit the floor
The Vic's you can remove, 'cause
I won't need them any more!

Reveille

I woke up from my fitful sleep
On fire and wet with need
The hunger raging through me, one
That only you could feed.

I felt your fingers on my breast
And then your tongue and lips
I writhed and moaned and could not still
The movement of my hips.

Your fingers traveled slowly down
But teased me on their way
I pleaded with you for release
Too hungry to delay.

You saw the state that I was in
And slid inside my heat
I shattered into tiny shards
My hands clenched in the sheet.

You held me then, our bodies flush
My cheek upon your heart
The love between us greater than
A poem can impart.

40-30-30

Better eat all your food now, baby
Finish up all of your greens
Better stock up on carbohydrates
So eat your potatoes and beans.

'Cause I've got all these plans made, baby
Sensual plans, all for you
I've been wanting to set them in motion
I don't think you'll mind if I do.

You'll be sweating and straining, baby
Moaning and asking for more
You'll be flexing your sexy muscles
And coming like never before.

When you're feeling quite sated, baby
Thinking you're due for some rest
I'll be sure to have Gatorade ready
Alpine Snow, as per your request.

By the time I am finished, baby
All of your strength will be gone
'Cause the plans that I have are to love you
Through the night and into the dawn.

So make sure you're ready, baby
Build up those glycogen stores
Take some vitamins, too, for good measure
Come in, baby. Then close the door.

Amen

Holy names tripped from off of my tongue
By the touch of your hands they were wrung
I'm a Jew, but to Jesus I called
Hope he wasn't too badly appalled
And I think God is my new best friend
His name issued forth time and again
I omitted Allah in my cries
Hope that lightning won't strike from the skies
But tell me, love, can it be true
That I didn't call your name out, too?

Come To Me

I suppose that by your work you've been detained
Leaving me with no release to be attained
I feel drunk though I have not been drinking wine
And I can't ignore the tingling in my spine.
It was cruel the way our phone call was cut off
And no longer at blue balls you'll hear me scoff
For I realize now that it all is true
I am close to going mad with lust for you!
So I'm wondering – perhaps you feel the same?
Do you need to come, love, calling out my name?
Do you want me half as much as I want you?
I need to take you and be taken, too.

I need to taste your body, north to south
I need to feel you coming in my mouth
And the thought of having your whole hand in me
Sets my mind to spinning, like I'm falling free.
But don't worry, love, it's not all in my mind
My body, heart and soul are all combined.
And I need you here with me, but I will wait
You and me together, love. It must be fate.

Hot To Trot

I'm hot to trot, I want some fun
I need your lovin' one on one
I want you, baby, in my arms
Where I can savor all your charms
Come here, I promise I won't bite
Unless you ask me to, all right?
So come and play with me tonight!

I'm hot to trot, I want some fun
I need your lovin' in the sun
I want to lie in meadows green
But somewhere where we won't be seen
And have you lie down by my side
To take me on a crazy ride
And make me feel so hot inside!

I'm hot to trot, I want some fun
I need your lovin' on the run
I want you, baby, in my car
So take me fast and take me far
We'll lean the seat back all the way
"Come get me, sweetheart," I will say
And hope the cops all stay away!

I'm hot to trot, I want some fun
Don't want to stop until I'm done
Until I've been so entertained
My stamina has all been drained
And though it goes against my grain
I'll rest a bit then from the strain
Until I'm set to start again!

I'm hot to trot, I want some fun
And baby, ours has just begun
'Cause while I'm taking that time out
We'll play a little turnabout
Then on the grass or in the Jeep
I'll take you hard and take you deep
And that's a promise I will keep!

On the Edge

Time seems to stop, on the edge of release
Skillfully teased with no hint of surcease
Sweating and straining, my breath coming fast
Rational thought now a thing of the past
Fingers inside me are reaching so deep
Filling a heart given into her keep
Soft words of love fall upon eager ears
Driving me onwards, as sweet release nears
One perfect touch and a scream rends the air
Pleasure sweeps through, almost too much to bear
Slowly relaxing, my hands loose their hold
Hints of a breeze on my flushed skin feel cold
Gathered up close in a loving embrace
Sleepy contentment spreads over my face
Nothing exists here except for us two
Resting securely in love strong and true.

Do You Know?

Do you know what you do to me
How your touches make me burn?
Do you know what it does to me
When you then respond in turn?
Do you know that I ache for you
How I need you deep within?
Can you tell I'm so wet for you
When your fingers touch my skin?
Do you know how I yearn for you
For your mouth to cover mine?
Do you know how I long for you
For your taste, as sweet as wine?
Do you know what I feel for you
How I'm overwhelmed with love?
Do you know you're a gift to me?
So much more than I dreamed of.

Hunger

I look at her with hungry eyes
The need I feel beyond disguise
Desire naked on my face
I long to be in her embrace
I want her fingers on my skin
I need to feel them reach within
I want to give up all control
To bare my heart and mind and soul
And give her everything; you see
She gives the very same to me

Halloween

I have you at my mercy at long last
But don't you worry, we'll both have a blast.
Where should I start, I wonder? I suppose
That first of all I'll take off all your clothes.
And when the final item is removed
Of what I see I know I will approve.
I'll walk you back until you hit the bed
And lay you down, your hands above your head
I'll have you clinging to the headboard tight
And then, my love, your passion I'll ignite.
I want you shaking, trembling with desire
I want your every cell to feel on fire
I want you incoherent, needing me
I want to hear you begging shamelessly.
And when I've had my fill of teasing you
When you feel that your release is long past due
I'll give you what you need; what I need, too
I'll take you hard and fast, that's what I'll do.
As you relax, I'll hold you in my arms
And pull the covers up to keep us warm.
But don't think we are done – oh no, my sweet
It's Halloween tonight, and you're my treat.

Thankful

I am thankful for your body
Grateful for its every part
That's a lot of thanks to give, and
I'm not sure where I should start.

I am thankful for your skin that
To my touch is soft and smooth
Some caresses will arouse it
Others still will serve to soothe.

I am thankful for your breasts and
For the nipples even more
With my mouth they have established
A most excellent rapport.

I am thankful for your legs that
Wrap around me as you come
Thighs that hold me even tighter
As to pleasure you succumb.

I am thankful for soft curls, but
More for what lies just below
And believe me I am grateful
My touch makes the juices flow!

I am thankful for your hands that
Touch me with unerring skill
And I voice those thanks quite loudly
As they fill me deeper still.

I am thankful for your mouth and
Let me not forget your tongue
It would be a lapse in manners
If its praises were not sung!

I am thankful for your arms that
Wrap me up and hold me tight
And especially the shoulder
That's my pillow for the night.

I am thankful for your eyes, in
Which the love shows strong and clear
What I see there keeps me going
Through the times when you're not near.

I am thankful for your body
Grateful for its every part
Most of all, my love, I'm thankful
That with me you've shared your heart.

Balance

Black leather cuffs fastened snug 'round my wrists
Nothing but naked emotion exists

Blindfolded, wondering what to expect
Flushed with arousal, my nipples erect

Facing the wall on my knees, can't hold still
Trembling with need as you tease me with skill

Feather-light touches with soft fingertips
Moans of frustration escaping my lips

Clenching down, feeling the wetness increase
Arching and twisting I beg for release

Total surrender, no shred of control
You're taking my body, I give you my soul.

Homage

Your body's laid out on the bed
Bare to my hot, hungry gaze
My eyes rake your sensual curves
I'm losing myself in a haze.

My hands have a mind of their own
Wandering over each part
They feel the hot pulse of your blood
The quickening pace of your heart.

I'm caught by the look in your eyes
Love showing clear in the blue
I feel my own heart beating hard
Full of emotion for you.

My fingers trace over your face
Luscious lips part on a sigh
This unending need that I feel
Is one I won't ever deny.

I follow the line of your throat
My lips have now joined in the fray
I scatter wet kisses along
Each inch of soft skin on my way.

Down between beautiful breasts
Leisurely breathing you in
Your heady scent stokes a desire
I feel in each pore of my skin.

Your nipples grow hard in my mouth
And under the touch of my hand
Your body's beginning to writhe
It knows every move I have planned.

Moving toward elegant legs
Silken smooth, soft inner thighs
With small, gentle bites of your skin
I'm slowly approaching my prize.

I feel your curls brushing my lips
Greedy, my mouth moves on you
Your hips arch, a desperate plea
I know what you want me to do.

Then spreading you open, I pause
Loving the wonderful view
Your body is flushed and aroused
I'm struck by the beauty that's you.

No teasing; I lower my head
Tasting the wetness I find
My mouth moves right up to your clit
My fingers are not far behind.

I feel you clench hard 'round my hand
Clit throbbing under my tongue
And knowing it's me loving you
Steals all the breath from my lungs.

I need you to come for me now
Give up every bit of control
I need you to call out my name
And give me your body and soul.

I'll gather you close in my arms
Cradle your head on my breast
Whisper my love in your ear
And feel you relax into rest.

Touch Me

Touch me, darling
Make me burn
Give me that for
Which I yearn.
Kiss me deeply
Breathe my air
Kiss me, darling
everywhere.
Stroke me gently
Tease my skin
Stroke me, darling
Deep within.
Take me hard and
Make me come
Take me, darling
I'll succumb.
Hold me to you
Very tight
Hold me, darling
Through the night.
Wake me slowly
With your kiss
Wake me, darling
Into bliss.

Chapter Three

Vines
(Vitis Vinifera)

Marathon! (At the Hop)

Bodies moving everywhere
The music's playing loud
Contagious moods of gaiety
Imbue the dancing crowd.

Beer in liberal amounts
Champagne, and even wine
I clink my plastic cup with yours
This evening you are mine.

Legs afire, my feet in pain
You drag me through the throng
To dance together, bodies close
As song fades into song.

People 'round us disappear
There's only you and me
Our eyes are locked, their message clear
Our need is plain to see.

Mouths are fused and tongues entwine
A sigh of utter bliss
Escapes me as I draw you near
And deepen our sweet kiss.

Aches forgotten, soreness gone
I'm floating on cloud nine
I know that when this evening's done
My love, you'll still be mine.

The 27th Mile

Another year, another twenty six point two are done
And honestly, I have to say it wasn't that much fun
I hurt in muscles that I didn't even know I had
The way I hobbled afterwards was really rather sad!

I waited for endorphins to kick in; alas, in vain
They never came, or else they were obscured by too much pain
The temperature was freezing cold, my tank-top much too thin
The chafe marks I developed stand out raw against my skin.

But if I had to choose to do it all again, or not
The answer would be simple; it would not require much thought
The aches are worth each kiss exchanged, so salty with our sweat
And finishing together hand in hand was better yet!

We wear our medals proudly, like survivors of a war
Each move we make reminds us that our bodies are still sore
And as we groan and grumble, cursing every step we ran
It's next year's hellish race that we already start to plan!

Again?!

Again my quads are screaming for relief
Again my tendons hurt beyond belief
Again I'm so exhausted I could cry
And once again I have to wonder, why?

What masochistic streak do I possess?
What foolish urge I can't seem to suppress
That has me at the starting line once more
Despite the knowledge of what lies in store?

Each little hill looms like Mount Everest
My poor heart hammers hard within my breast
The finish line seems miles and miles away
I realize it *is*, to my dismay.

The crowds I run past yell, "You're looking strong!"
They're well intentioned liars and they're wrong!
That grimace on my face is not a smile
As painfully I run another mile.

But then, at last I cross the finish line
(The tape is long since gone, but I don't mind)
The agony is done for one more race
A weary smile is spreading on my face.

I have the medal and the T-shirt, too
They're over now, those twenty-six point two
In time the aches and pains will all be gone
And I'll prepare for next year's marathon!

A Poet, Don't You Know It

You write down every hackneyed thought that flits across your mind
And you're absolutely certain that your words are so refined
Then to poesy.com you sent your latest works of art
Oh my God, a semi-finalist – be still my beating heart!

Your unique artistic vision was by far beyond compare
Now you call yourself a poet with a grave, distinguished air.
But to make completely sure, you post your poetry online
And receive conclusive feedback that your writing is divine.

If the meter tends to wander here and there, or everywhere
Well, the judges on that website, they just didn't seem to care!
And the rhymes which sound a bit contrived? The words that don't make sense?
That's just your own unique technique, you say in your defense.

Hey, so what if there are typos – two or three, or even more?
You're a poet of the people, not an academic bore!
When the Muse is feeling frisky, that's what really matters, Mac
Write it down in sixty seconds, turn the page and don't look back.

So of course, these wondrous poems must not languish in the dark
On the noble quest of publishing you're ready to embark!
After all, your online readers have all told you that you're great
And you've promised them signed copies of the book – but they pay freight.

Move on over, Milton! Buzz off, Blake! Your time has long since passed
There's a new kid on the block now, one whose verse is unsurpassed.
So farewell, Frost! Later, Lorca! Sayonara, Percy Bysshe!
For to write with such artistic vision, you could only wish!

Sex in Iambic Heptameter

I tried to write a love scene for my two protagonists
My words, however, made them seem like two antagonists
They grappled and they clutched; their mouths were locked as in a duel
Instead of tender love-making, it all seemed rather cruel.

I tore my draft to pieces and I threw it in the trash
And started over, sure that I could do it in a flash
The muse was clearly with me as my words flowed on the screen
But when I read the scene I turned a sickly shade of green!

"She slid inside the sopping hole and stroked the swollen bud"
And: "Pressing on the magic button, felt the liquid flood"
All honey-pots and oysters, gushing nectar, oozing juice
Some passion-pits and pussies, too, their essence flowing loose.

I tore the second draft as well, and burned it in the fire
There has to be a way, I thought, to write of real desire!
I need to steer my writing clear of these bizarre clichés
And try to use more common words and simple turns of phrase.

The muse was being good to me, my words flowed forth again
I wrote without a pause until my fingers cramped in pain
But once again, reviewing how I'd written the affair
I groaned and gnashed my teeth and threw my hands up in despair!

The passion-pits had given way; vaginas took their place
Not honey-pots or oysters, but a perineal space
The clitoris and labia were stroked just so, but then
It sounded like a visit to the OB-GYN!

The third draft hit the trash post-haste, but now I stopped to think
No point in rushing onwards if the end-result would stink
I pondered and reflected, then at last I saw the light
And realized exactly what to do to get it right.

They say "Write what you know about," which leads me to deduce
The only course of action is to practice self-abuse
But every time I do I get so caught up in myself
The story lies unfinished where I left it on the shelf!

Taking the Plunge

If a dive into the waters of self-pity you desire
If a dip in abject misery is all that you require
Step right up now, don't be shy, and let me tell you how it's done
You can do it any time of day, but late night is most fun!

You don't need external props, it's all about your state of mind
If you dig into your psyche, surely some excuse you'll find
Once the reason has been found, just follow this one simple rule:
Close your eyes and say out loud, "there's no place like the pity pool."

If you want to, tap your heels; whatever helps you in your task
For myself, I find it never hurts to dip into my flask
Then I chant a well-known litany to help me set the mood
All about how things are so unfair, and how my life is screwed.

Well, I think I've covered everything, so now it's up to you
Please don't hesitate to call me if there's something I can do
One more thing I hope you'll do, unless you're something of a fool
Have a good friend standing by to kick your ass out of that pool!

You've Got SPAM!

"You too, Em Reed, can now enlarge your penis, click this link!"
They don't know mine is silicone, a lovely shade of pink.
"Increase your breast size without risk, it's natural and safe!"
But if I did, my running bra would more than likely chafe.
"Click here for free Viagra, no prescription is required!"
But I don't need their help; my baby always keeps me fired.
"Hot chicks in triple X positions, look at them for free!"
But plastic breasts and vacant eyes don't do that much for me.
"Free printer ink for sale, and now the cartridges are cheap!"
But I don't own a printer, so their stock I'll let them keep.
"Em Reed, lose 10 pounds in 10 days, but hurry, please act now!"
But even if I wanted to, I doubt they'd tell me how.
"Buy Norton Antivirus for 10 bucks, protect yourself!"
Thank God I work with Unix, it can take care of itself.
It seems each message I report spawns more to take its place
But I'm an e-mail addict, so the onslaught I'll embrace!

Insomnia

I couldn't sleep, I tossed and turned
As night gave way to dawn
My love, she was oblivious
And slumbered deeply on.

Her features were relaxed in sleep
With slightly parted lips
I pulled the covers gently down
Just barely past her hips.

My hand skimmed over sexy curves
I felt my body stir
Her soft moan left me confident
Of what would next occur.

But then she turned away from me
And pulled the covers high
She slumbered on, quite undisturbed
Alas! Not so was I.

Dr. J

I sing an ode to Dr. J
There's nothing like a shot a day
Well, maybe two or three or four
In fact, I think I'd best do more!
Now, Dr. J, he's not some fake
He'll minister to every ache
So every time I'm feeling blue
I'll turn to whiskey, tried and true!
A shot or two will start me off
I'm past the novice choking cough
And when I reach the seventh shot
Oh baby, I'm so hot to trot!
I sing an ode to Dr. J
I preach to you the whiskey way
So if you're troubled, sad and blue
Just turn to whiskey, tried and true!

Ode to a Speculum

Oh speculum, my speculum
Come enter me with grace
Your cold unfeeling metal touch
My poor heart sets to race!

Without the least care or concern
You push my lips aside
Exposed for all the world to see
You spread me open wide.

I dream about you weeks before
We actually meet
But when I see you on the tray
I dream about retreat.

Oh speculum, my speculum
Don't be offended, dear
I don't think I could handle you
Much more than once a year!

Femme I Am!

I am Femme
Femme-I-am

That Femme-I-am!
That Femme-I-am!
I do not like
that Femme-I-am

Do you like
Long polished nails?

I do not like them,
Femme-I-am.
I don't want nails like some Madame's.

Would you like them in bright red?

No, I would not in bright red.
They would be hard to use in bed.
I don't want nails like some Madame's
I do not like them, Femme-I-am!

Would you like them manicured?
Would you like your hangnails cured?

I would not want them manicured
To your ideas I am inured
I would not like them in bright red,
I would not be caught with them dead.
I don't want nails like some Madame's
I do not like them, Femme-I-am!

Would you like stiletto heels?
A dress that every curve reveals?

I would not like stiletto heels
I hate to think of how that feels
I could not, would not, wear a dress
I would be in a state of stress
I do not want a manicure
The very thought I can't endure
I do not want them in bright red
I'd rather have them short instead
I don't want nails like some Madame's
I do not like them, Femme-I-am!

You do not want these things, you say
Try them, try them, and you may!
Try them, and you may, I say!

Femme, if you will let me be
I will try them. You will see....

Say!
I like long polished nails!
They leave the most intriguing trails!
And I would like them in bright red
Please paint them now, Femme, go ahead!
And I would like a manicure
I even want a pedicure!
And I will wear stiletto heels
A dress that all my curves reveals!
I do want nails like some Madame's,
I do so like them, Femme-I-am
Thank you!
Thank you!
Femme-I-am!!

Online Blues

I'd been waiting online
For that woman of mine
I had pinged her five times
Heard Yahoo!'s grating chimes
But the screen remained blank
And I felt my hopes tank.

I could only conclude
That tonight's interlude
Would, alas, be delayed
My desire unallayed.

And the webcam showed black
So I gave it a whack
But all that did was cause
My own broadcast to pause
And I looked rather green
On the laptop's small screen.

I was pissed off by then
So I whacked it again
And I gave it a kick
This, it seems, did the trick.

Then I pinged her again
And I counted to ten
No reply was returned
And I felt sad and spurned
But although I felt blue
I did not close Yahoo!

So I set off to bed
With a slow, heavy tread
When I suddenly heard
That a ping had occurred!

As I ran quickly back
I stepped smack on a tack
But ignoring the pain
Faced my laptop again
And with bright, eager eyes
Felt my dampened hopes rise.

Then my curses flowed free
For I saw who'd pinged me
Not my woman – oh, no
But my mom, don't you know!

Oh, how stupid was that
Having taught her to chat?
I was so hopping mad
I did something real bad
Kicked the wall hard and fast
Now my leg's in a cast.

And my love, where was she
While this happened to me?
She had fallen asleep
And had not heard a peep!

Reaper

When I die I'll be awake
My soul won't be the Lord's to take
I'll stare the Reaper in the eye
And follow him, my head held high
Then he will lead me straight to hell
Where I'll have been condemned to dwell.
My toasty fate I won't bemoan
For all my choices are my own
And even if they lead to hell
I know I will have lived life well.

Chapter Four

Figs
(Ficus Carica)

Forbidden Fruit

The feel of your lips on mine lingers
As does the touch of your fingers
The taste of your skin is so clear
Wondrous, as I drew you near
Much later my pulse is still pounding
Echoes of need still resounding
These images run through my mind
I'm edgy; can't seem to unwind
I need you to stop the onslaught
Show me again what you've taught
Forbidden fruit, heady as wine
Sweeter than honey, divine
Enlightenment truly is mine
I see now, where once I was blind
I see what it is that I'll miss
The magic I found in your kiss.

Demons

Too many nights crying too many tears
Nothing allays these insidious fears.
Spreading like poison, polluting my veins
Attacking my mind in a vicious campaign.

Squeezing me hard with each breath that I take
Patiently stalking, awaiting the break.
Perfidious warfare waged deep in the dark
Taking its toll on me, leaving its mark.

Shredded to pieces, my sanity lost
Unbearably heavy the ultimate cost.
Nowhere to run now, no place left to hide
The demons that dog me, I carry inside.

Pyrite

Like the children of Israel
Who longed for the flesh pots
Forgetting the shackles
That held them too tight
Afraid of the burden
That freedom had brought.

A freedom so yearned for
Utopian, flawless
While still an unreachable dream.

Yet now it draws near
And it closes in on me
With measured, implacable strides
A fearsome reality
That finds me craving
Captivity's gold-plated cage.

In Limbo

Not strong enough to leave, and yet
Not weak enough to stay
Another bit eroding with
The passing of each day.

The good I can't remember and
The bad I can't forget
Sound loudly in my head and drown
The soft voice of regret.

The promise of a better life
A siren's call I heed
But who will suffer in my wake
Left silently to bleed?

Dark eyes that haunt my sleep at night
They cannot understand
They cling to what they can, and keep
A death grip on my hand.

The tears I can't seem to contain
Persist in asking why
The answer never good enough
To justify the lie.

No Return

Past the point of no return
See how bright my bridges burn
See the thick smoke billow out
Obfuscating any doubt
See the haze imbue the air
With heavy tendrils of despair
See the ashes coat the ground
Burying grave sorrow's sound.

Out of Sorts

I'm feeling out of sorts
Uneasy in my skin
Can't seem to settle down
Disquiet churns within.

Dark clouds accumulate
The sky is overcast
The mood outside as foul
As mine, these long months past.

The storm is coming now
And lightning flashes bright
With howling rage it pounds
Throughout the cold, long night.

As dawn dispels the dark
You'll see, by morning's light
The wreckage of my life
And dreams that won't take flight.

The Midas Touch

I have the Midas touch of pain
My fingers burn like acid rain
Inflicting hurt on those I love
A curse from some cruel god above
My good intentions mock me so
They show the woman that I know
I want to be, whose touch brings joy
Who doesn't know how to destroy
The life of one whose only crime
Was loving her so long a time.
I have the Midas touch of pain
The blood of wounds I've caused has stained
My hands, and colored them in red
So dark, that even tears have fled
As I look on, eyes cold and dry
Incapable of a reply
When asked the single question: why?
And all around me people say
That they'd be wise to stay away
But not a one can understand
That I am burned by my own hand.

Enough!

Enough! I cannot measure up
To what you all expect
It's time I thought about myself
And found some self-respect.

Enough of being your support
The anchor for your fears
Of not expressing what I need
For far too many years.

Enough of trying to explain
And needing to defend
Of feeling disappointed that
You will not comprehend.

Enough of needing to appear
Secure and strong to you
Of trying not to let the grief
And rage I feel show through.

Enough of expectations
Be they real or in my mind
It's time I thought about myself
And left them all behind.

Critical Point

Boiling, building
Hot and heavy
Bubbling deep within
Coiling, pulsing
Flowing near
The surface of my skin.

Ice-cold fury
Red-hot rage
Run molten in my veins
Burning me
Consuming me
And weakening the chains.

Voice of reason
Ever dimmer
Swallowed in the din
Phase transition
Sane to mad
Now Chaos will begin.

C'est La Vie

Life is real; it's not a fairy tale
Where true love conquers all
And the sad truth is that sometimes
You cannot avoid the fall.

Life is all about commitments
And responsibility
Seeking happiness – a painful
Lesson in futility.

Life is all about the choices
You must make, at such high cost
Does a quiet conscience compensate
For love that has been lost?

Life is real; it's not a fairy tale
Where happy endings rule
And yet my heart won't give up hope
Proclaiming me a fool.

Choice

Choice is illusion
The ultimate lie
A fiction created
To help you get by.

To make you believe
That you have some control
Falling head first
Down the white rabbit's hole.

But somewhere inside
A small voice you can't quell
Insists on the truth
And it rings like a knell.

Choice is illusion
The ultimate lie
Life sweeps you away
Until someday you die.

Disillusionment

"You're confused," so she said, and it cut like a knife
From the mouth of the one who had given me life
And I gaped at the phone, and I couldn't believe
And I hoped against hope that my ears had deceived.
"And your children," she said, "they should not be with you"
The conviction she felt coming quite clearly through
And the shock stole my voice, momentarily mute
As I searched for some words that her claims would refute.
Though I knew that my words fell on stubborn, deaf ears
Still I tried to explain, in a voice choked with tears.
But the sense of betrayal was deep in my bones
And I knew there was no way that she could atone
In the span of five minutes so much damage done
Trust built over the years was now suddenly gone.
And yet try as I might not to care, not to cry
She's my mother, I love her, this I can't deny.

Boyling

When pressure increases the volume decreases
As long as the temperature's set
At this rate I won't have to wait too much longer
Before I implode on myself
The pressure seems quite isotropic in nature
From every direction at once
Symmetrically pushing unfailingly inwards
It forces the air from my lungs
My feeble attempts to push back are all futile
And weaken me more with each try
The pressure is squeezing my eyes, unrelenting
Perhaps that explains why I cry.

Shepherd

The Lord is my shepherd, I shall not want
For misery, sorrow and grief
His guidance in life is my unjust reward
For the many long years of belief.

The Lord is my shepherd, I shall not fear
Though I walk in the valley of death
His presence the coldest of comforts to me
When it's time to exhale my last breath.

Salva Me

Lie down beside me and hold me so tight
Keep the demons at bay on this dark stormy night
Rock me to sleep as I cry in your arms
Grant me somnolence sweet as my soul slowly warms
Shelter, protect me from what lies ahead
From a tortuous path I do not want to tread
Lend me the courage to do what I must
I can face down my demons when armed with your trust
Love me 'til dawn breaks and red tints the sky
Send me forth to the fray by your love fortified
Battle scarred, weary, returning to you
Promise clear in your eyes of a life starting new
Tears of relief cleanse my face as I cry
I know that you love me and need not ask why.

Graveyard

Beneath that headstone, over there
I buried all my dreams
And this white stone, right here, is where
I stifled all my screams
Another splendid marble tomb
Holds all my hopes within
And one with contents yet unknown
The cost for all my sins.

Hindsight

Those who've loved with all their hearts
And ultimately lost
Must wonder, "was it worth it?"
When they realize the cost.

For when the scales have settled
And the pain outweighs the gain
The memory of what might have been
Is all that will remain.

Wheels

I want to tell you that things will work out
To silence the clamorous voices of doubt
But how, when I really don't know that it's true
Don't know when or even if I'll be with you?
It feels like I'm drowning, I've run out of air
I'm searching for answers that aren't really there
I'm tired of feeling so needy and weak
I'm scared when I see how the future looms bleak.
Afraid of the day you at last realize
You can look at me clearly, without biased eyes
And decide that you've had quite enough of it all
Of holding me up and preventing my fall.
I'm all out of gas, but the wheels? They still spin
The demons inside still maniacally grin.

Tick Tock

Ticking softly
Ever present
Waiting down the road
Counting backwards
Unrelenting
Waiting to explode
Borrowed minutes
Ever fleeting
Coming to an end
Devastation
On a scale too
Large to comprehend
One goodbye leads
To another
Till there's no hello
Ticking softly
Time's run out, and
Swept us in its flow.

In Time

In time all things will be as they should be
And love will triumph, bringing with it light
Though every sunrise heralds a new fight
Where blows rain down upon me ceaselessly
Though hopelessness is close to claiming me
I cling to one faint hope with all my might
In time all things will be as they should be
And love will triumph, bringing with it light.

Like so much flotsam, swept away to sea
So hope has fled from me, far out of sight
Escaping under cover of the night.

And yet one tiny piece remains with me
In time all things will be as they should be.

Scars

Ephemeral, faint
Disappearing too swiftly
The shattered remains of a dream
A fantasy lost
Though the hope lingers on, and
Refuses to leave me in peace.
Your mark on my skin
Is a constant reminder
That love cannot win against life
Our choices were made
And reality banished
The dream we had hoped to live out.

In Vain

I flipped the bedroom light switch on
Not quite believing you were gone
The rumpled cotton sheets still kept
An imprint of you where you'd slept
The faintest odor in the air
Reminded me of what we'd shared
And then it hit me in the gut
Far sharper than a knife, it cut
A wave of loneliness so deep
And sweeping that I could not keep
From calling out your name in pain
Although I knew it was in vain.

Full Circle

Too short a time I burned, too brief the flame
But while it flared the sun could not compete
Now only embers glow, the fire is banked
For lack of air will always mean defeat.

Soon all the red will fade to cold black ash
The cinders of a love that blazed too hot
Another fire will slowly burn away
The memories, and I will be forgot.

Revelation

So this is grief.

Wrenching, crippling pain
Searing through my skin
Tearing through my heart
Ripping me apart.

I never knew.

Silent, anguished tears
Acid on my face
Burning through my soul
Gaping, aching holes.

But now I do.

Dreary, hazy days
Sleepless, endless nights
Hollow, empty life
Missing you. But I

Have no regrets.

Cheers

I raise my glass to misery
I drink a toast to pain
I've been here countless times before
I may as well again.
Another, and another, till
The pain begins to blur
Until the sorrow all spills out
And speech begins to slur.
Besieged defenses fall, and
The façade cracks open wide
As grief and rage pour through me, and
I cannot stem the tide.
I say to her, then, in my mind
The things she'll never hear
Let out the nightmares haunting me
The paralyzing fear.
And when the storm abates at last
I'm left exposed and bare
But not a God-damned thing has changed
The pain is still right there.

Faith

My faith, it sometimes wanders
In the stillness of the night
When the solitude surrounds me
And exhausts my will to fight.

When your voice is not enough
To hold the rising fears at bay
And I see that there's no answer
To the fervent prayers I pray.

When I worry I'll forget
The special way you look at me
When I reach my hand to touch
But cannot touch a memory.

In these dark and silent hours
When the ache consumes me whole
All I have is battered faith
The glue that holds my shattered soul.

The Flip Side

Sweet are poets' songs that to the might of love are sung
But bitter is the taste of salty tears upon my tongue.

Loudly those in love proclaim the joy of being whole
But quiet is the loneliness that cuts into my soul.

Soothing is the lover's touch that heals the wounded heart
But cold as death the distance keeping you and me apart.

Verses on the joy of love come quickly and with ease
But silent is the pain of love, which nothing can appease.

Dawn

As gnawing, clawing terror infiltrates
Insidiously claiming every part
Invading every chamber of my heart
As penetrating fear breaks down my gates
The voice of reason promptly abdicates
And sense and logic hasten to depart.
Then demons their grim prophecies impart
As crushing darkness through me radiates.
But words of love you utter pierce the veil
The dark is vanquished, banished by your light
The demons flee with one last angry wail
And sanity is once again in sight.
For through these trials, our love *will* prevail
A beacon in the darkness, shining bright.

Hypnagogic

I dreamed last night that she was gone
And I was left alone
Distraught and panicky I tried
To call her on the phone.

I woke up with a startled gasp
Soaked through with sweat and dread
So vivid was the dream, I thought
I'd be alone in bed.

But then I turned my head and saw
Her silent, sleeping form
I reached a shaking hand to touch
Her shoulder. It was warm.

I curled into her body as
My heart slowed down its pace
She wasn't gone, and I could sleep
Secure in her embrace.

Missing You

I miss you so badly tonight
I miss the soft sound of your voice
I miss the sweet touch of your hands
I miss you, and it was my choice.

And it's hurting and burning
Consuming me whole
And it's clawing inside me
Corroding my soul.

I need you to say it's okay
To say it will all be all right
I need you to rock me to sleep
Wrapped up in your arms for the night.

But you're not here to catch me
You're not here to see
And you're not here to hold me
To answer my plea.

I wonder how long I can last
Before I admit I can't cope
I wonder if we'll see the day
We finally live out our hope.

But I will not give up, love
I want you to know
That I love you so much, and
I won't let you go.

Don't Give Up

When the bed is cold and lonely
And the distance seems too great
When it looks like we won't make it
And despair waits at the gate.

When my voice is not enough to
Keep the rising fears at bay
When you need a lover's touch, but
I'm a million miles away.

When you're ready to give up, and
Think you cannot last the day
When you look to me for comfort, but
There's nothing I can say.

Don't you give up on us, baby
Don't you know we're meant to be?
And throughout the time apart, love
You're the only one for me.

Just remember that I love you
Like you've never known before
That I cherish and adore you
And I will forever more.

Regrets

Our mortality nips at our heels
But fools that we are, we ignore it
We see it strike out at our friends
And then we decry and abhor it.

We squander our time on this earth
We waste precious moments we're given
But thinking of her at death's door
I wonder. By what are we driven?

By plans to accumulate cash
By living for others' opinion
By hoping to live out our dreams
Before we approach Death's dominion.

But the future is not guaranteed
And Death lies around the next corner
I don't want to die with regrets
I cry for myself as I mourn her.

Chapter 5

Olives
(Olea Europea)

Ashes to Ashes

Ashes to ashes and dust to dust
Whence we came, there we return
Six million innocents, before their time
In the fires of hatred they burned

Ashes to ashes and dust to dust
Under ominous skies of grey
Thick smoke billowing out their lives
To a merciless God they prayed.

Ashes to ashes and dust to dust
Scattered by indifferent winds
Little feet silenced forevermore
Too young to ever have sinned.

Ashes to ashes and dust to dust
As a silent world looked on
Nothing left of the innocent dead
Their memory almost gone.

Ashes to ashes and dust to dust
Whence we came, there we return
Six million call from beyond the grave
We speak that the world will learn.

Thieves

You took my money
You took my clothes
I tried to fight
You rained down blows
You took my food
You took my drink
You beat me so
I could not think
You jammed me in
A cattle car
I couldn't move
It traveled far
You took my hair
And my gold teeth
You left me nothing
To bequeath
You took my name
Tattooed my skin
A life of terror
To begin
You took my air
You gave me smoke
My mother's ashes
Made me choke
You made me put them
In the fire
And death awaited
Should I tire
You stole my life
You had no right
But I survived
That monstrous night
You killed six million
Of my kin
But in the end
You couldn't win.

Punch Cards

Six million numbers, holes in a punch card
No names, only numbers in blue
Soulless machines running twenty-four/seven
Punch hole number 8 for the Jew.

Indexed and sorted, cross-indexed, resorted
Each drop of blood traced to its source
Every cog oiled and kept running smoothly
No time and no use for remorse.

Corporate greed and insane racial hatred
A merger of murder and Marks
Six million numbers, the people who burned
In a windfall of ashes and sparks.

Another Day

Another day, another bombing
Another young boy dead
Another bus that's blown to pieces
Another street runs red.

Another day, another headline
Another list of names
Another special news announcement
Broadcast from the flames.

Another useless condemnation
And laying of the blame
Another day, still no solution
To terror's deadly game.

Roulette

Only one old man killed
Exhaled sighs of relief
Look how calloused we are
How selective our grief.

Dozens wounded today
But as yet we're ahead
On the scoreboard of blood
Where we tally the dead.

Scan the paper for names
Was it someone you knew?
Carry on with your life
Not much else you can do.

Let's play Russian Roulette
Dare we get on a bus?
Will the next Breaking News
Broadcast pieces of us?

Shaheed

They kill with such impunity
No reverence for life
The bastards use what tools they can
The bomb, the gun, the knife
They wage a war of terror, vile
Their only goal to kill
So easy not to think as blood
Of innocents they spill
They wage their bloody "holy" war
They want to be Shaheed
Just kill some children, blow them up
A simple task, indeed
Does Allah wait with open arms
These bastards to embrace?
Well, he can have them all right now
And leave us not a trace.

Milk and Honey

It's the land of milk and honey
That was promised us of old
Here your death arrives at lunchtime
As your food is getting cold.

She is sitting at the table
On her hands she leans her head
If you didn't know what happened
You would never guess she's dead.

Do you see that plastic bag here
In the stroller, by the door?
That's a baby lying in there
But he won't cry anymore.

It's the land of milk and honey
Stained with blood of innocents
Here your death comes unexpected
And it never makes much sense.

Our Time

It's been far too long in coming
After decades lived in fear
But the winds of change are blowing
Different times, at last, are here.

Now it's sweeping through the country
And this tide will *not* be stemmed
Even though by narrow-minded
Right-wing bigots we're condemned.

Though the war will be a hard one
Uphill battles all the way
There is hope to help sustain us
As we look around today.

All you people in the shadows
Come and join us in the light
Yes, the war is far from over
But we just might win this fight.

Innocence

I want to wrap him in my arms
And never let him go
Protect him from the world outside
The pain he's sure to know.
His eyes hold only innocence
Such confidence and trust
I wish that he could stay this way
But change will come; it must.
In time he'll learn that people lie
Use others for their needs
Manipulate and cheat and hate
Do terrifying deeds.
His eyes will lose their innocence
They'll gain a guarded look
They'll show the pain of lessons learned
And of the blows he took.
And I will feel them as my own
Each hurt etched on his face
I'll cry for him and ache for him
And wish to take his place.
But all of that is years ahead
He's still a boy today
And as I hold him close to me
I hold the world at bay.

Into Sleep

With tousled hair
And sleepy eyes
'Tween sleep and wakefulness
He lies.

A small hand strokes
His faithful bear
It's frayed and worn
He doesn't care.

A soft exhale
Now eyes are closed
So innocent
In his repose.

A light kiss planted
On his brow
When he's awake
He won't allow.

I close the door
And dim the light
With one last kiss
I bid goodnight.

Chapter 6

Wheat and Barley
(Triticum Aestivum and *Horduem Vulgare)*

Party Girls

I bring fresh flowers to the grave on every Halloween
Bright tulips were her preference, with ferns of vibrant green
I stand before the headstone that proclaims her date of death
Recalling vividly the moment when she last drew breath.

You shake your head in puzzlement, I'm sure, at what I say
So listen closely as I tell my story, if I may
It started but three years ago, when first I saw her face
Maneuvering around the crowd with captivating grace.

All eyes were on her; men were gawking, women stared in awe
A vision clad in red and black: exquisite, not a flaw
I knew for certain, at that moment, she would soon be mine
And when she took my proffered arm I saw it as a sign.

She danced with me that evening and our bodies moved as one
The brilliance of her gaze eclipsing that of any sun
All eyes were fixed on me, intently taking in the scene
Oh, how they wished that they could take my place that Halloween!

What followed was an idyll of romantic, fated love
In her I knew I'd found the woman I'd been dreaming of
With solemn oaths, we swore that to each other we'd be true
I meant to keep my vows, and I was sure that she would, too.

My sweet, why did you have to go and leave me all alone?
A lock of hair is all I have, the rest beneath the stone
And on its head are etched the words "I loved you so, my dear"
If things had just been different she would not be lying here.

You see, my friend, it's evident that I am not to blame
They gathered in her shadow and to her it was a game
I might have not been present for all anyone would care
She tantalized and tempted; it was more than I could bear

I used to be the one that people looked for in a crowd
To be seen in my presence was a reason to be proud
But bit by bit I noticed it was her they would surround
Ignoring my existence, it was her they swarmed around.

An easy smile upon her lips, a carefree attitude
She basked in the attention, leaving me in solitude.
The men were gawking and the women stared at her with awe
She teased them with seductive looks that scraped my feelings raw.

Yet that was not the worst of what awaited me that night
As I stood near her stoically, a shadow to her light
She turned to me coquettishly and asked me for some wine
I made my way toward the bar and took my place in line.

But as I headed back to take my place there at her side
My eyes were met with such a sight my heart could not abide
It pains me to recall her grievous sin to this day still
Please, ask no more of me, for of the dead I won't speak ill.

It fell on Halloween, a full year from our first embrace
And not a single soul then wished to be there, in my place
I stood and watched as she betrayed me and destroyed my life
And felt the white-hot rage as it seared through me like a knife.

That night in bed she turned from me and feigned exhausted sleep
I smiled and thought "No matter, from now on you're mine to keep."
I pressed the pillow to her face and pinned her to the bed
And "Happy Anniversary, our first and last," I said.

Her thrashing slowly dwindled and at last the deed was done
I looked at her and checked for signs of life, but there were none
I drew her to me closely and I held her through the night
Her body cooled and stiffened as the dark gave way to light.

I called for the police and spoke with panic and distress
The officers interrogated me without success
The coroner decreed that she had died of cause unknown
And offered his condolences that I was left alone.

I chose a lovely headstone and the funeral was grand
It all came off without a hitch, exactly as I'd planned.
I've moved on with my life; I hardly think of her at all
Except for once a year: I bring her flowers every fall.

Now, there across the graveyard, she is waiting by the gate
I met her at a party; I was sure it must be fate
She wore—was it coincidence?—a dress of red and black
I caught her eye and knew that there could be no going back.

I see the way you gaze at her, enchanted by her face
I see you notice how she walks, with elegance and grace
She's reveling in your attention, look how wide her smile
And see the way she sways her hips, to taunt you and beguile.

I've been her lover these three months and fear she doesn't see
She's stealing the attention that by right belongs to me
Already people flock to her, my presence they ignore
I think this grave has room enough to hold one woman more....

In Her Image

The days were cold and windy, winter's chill hung in the air
The sky was grey and overcast, the trees stood starkly bare
The ground was hard and frozen, dead grass scattered here and there
And fallen leaves blew in the wind, away to who knows where.

The town lay still beneath a heavy covering of snow
Its silent, empty streets seemed to reflect an eerie glow
The houses were all tightly shut to fend against the storm
The curtains drawn, the fires lit, to keep the townsfolk warm.

A woman walked the cobbled streets, intent upon her path
Consumed by overwhelming grief and full of righteous wrath
The image of her lover's lifeless body filled her mind
Before her death she'd suffered horrors of the vilest kind.

Her crime was love, a kind the townsfolk couldn't understand
Two women living on their own, alone, without a man
Although, disturbing not a soul, they went about their way
Intolerance and ignorance would not be held at bay.

One evening, after too much ale, three young men formed a plan
To show the women what it meant to spurn a handsome man
They stalked the one until at last they cornered her alone
And when she saw their faces she let out a frightened moan.

She cried and begged for mercy, but the men did not relent
Made bold by ale, they didn't stop until their lust was spent
Her cries grew slowly weaker as at last her movements stilled
They left her there for dead, their wicked urges now fulfilled.

The woman waiting in their house grew more and more concerned
The hour was getting late and still her mate had not returned
A sinking feeling in her stomach twisted like a knife
As finally she set out looking for her missing wife.

She came upon a figure lying naked in the street
Its limbs were torn and twisted and the blood pooled by its feet
Her broken cry of disbelief and anguish split the air
She knelt beside her wife, and touched the battered face with care.

She whispered words of hope and comfort to her injured wife
But knew that within minutes there would be no sign of life
A final effort then, as bloodied lips spoke one more time
And told the woman who it was that took part in the crime.

The grieving, broken-hearted woman went to the police
The guilty men were brought before the justice of the peace
Then in a shaky voice she told her story to the court
Believing, in her innocence, that she would find support.

The young men who had done the deed were sons of wealthy folk
So justice passed them by when money eloquently spoke
The woman watched in disbelief as guilty men walked free
While headed out the courtroom doors they sneered at her with glee.

She walked back to her house with aching heart and heavy feet
No more her lover at the door with kisses would she greet
The darkened windows seemed an air of mourning to convey
No fire crackled in the hearth to drive the chill away.

That night she lay alone in bed enshrouded in her grief
She couldn't shed a single tear, she couldn't find relief
She hugged her lover's pillow to her, closing weary eyes
But still she saw the grisly image of her wife's demise.

For many days she mourned the death of her beloved mate
She couldn't sleep, she couldn't eat, her grief would not abate
Half-crazed with pain she wandered to and fro about the house
And everywhere she looked she saw reminders of her spouse.

Her face was gaunt, her body thin, her eyes had lost their spark
With every passing day her thoughts grew bleaker and more dark
Without her lover by her side she found no joy in life
And contemplated whether it was time to join her wife.

Then in her troubled mind resurfaced fragments of a tale
She'd heard it as a girl, and now remembered one detail
She thought upon it constantly and dreamed of it at night
And wondered if the storyteller possibly was right.

The storyteller used to come quite frequently to town
A gypsy with a weathered face that never seemed to frown
The children, eager for a tale, would gather all around
And ask to hear of magic deeds and treasures lost and found.

The townsfolk didn't know how old she was, or whence she came
She spoke not of herself and no one even knew her name
She lived beyond the outskirts of the town, a distance fair
And not a single person from the town had ventured there.

She'd wander through the cobbled streets in worn and tattered rags
With homemade goods to sell and trade in ancient, battered bags
"The Gypsy," so they called her, in a condescending tone
They let her tell her tales and left her pretty much alone.

But sometimes as she walked through town she'd stop a passerby
She'd lay a wrinkled hand on his, an odd gleam in her eye
Then in a hollow voice she'd speak of strange and sundry things
And stranger still, at times she'd speak of future happenings.

At first the townsfolk thought she wasn't quite right in the head
But over time they noticed things would happen as she'd said
Their scorn and condescension turned to superstitious fear
It wasn't long before they didn't want her coming near.

Whenever she appeared in town in anger they would curse
And make crude gestures meant demonic spirits to disperse
The merchants in the shops refused to sell her any wares
And where she went she felt the weight of hateful, fearful stares.

But when the children too began to jeer and curse and shout
She knew her storytelling days were done beyond a doubt
The gypsy's visits to the town grew few and far between
At length they stopped and years went by without her being seen.

The woman had been just a child when all this had occurred
She'd listened to the gypsy, hanging onto every word
And now she wondered if at last she'd gone quite mad with grief
For putting faith in tales she knew were wild beyond belief.

And yet, she couldn't help but feel a spark of hope ignite
Recalling how the gypsy seemed possessed of second sight
Perhaps there *was* some truth in all those tales the gypsy told
Perhaps there *was* a way to free her wife from death's dark hold.

She quickly brushed her tangled hair and dressed haphazardly
Then headed forth to where she thought the gypsy's house would be
Her stomach churned, her heart beat fast, her palms were slick with sweat
The wild hope she was feeling drove her onward, faster yet.

She left the town behind and walked past fields of corn and hay
And walked on, even when she thought she must have lost her way
Then suddenly she saw the house atop a little rise
A welcome sight to weary legs and gritty, burning eyes.

But as she neared the house she saw neglect had spread throughout
And felt the tiny spark of hope she'd nursed replaced by doubt
The windows all were boarded shut, the paint was chipped away
And in the yard were weeds and thorns that grew in disarray.

The woman thought the gypsy must have died some years before
But still she climbed the creaking steps and faced the wooden door
She raised her hand to knock, but froze mid-motion, terrified
For on its own, it seemed, the heavy door swung open wide.

Her heartbeat, which had seemed to stop, resumed a frantic pace
She turned white as a sheet, the shock etched clearly on her face
The storyteller stood before her disbelieving eyes
And when the gypsy's hand caught hers she started in surprise.

The gypsy spoke then, and her voice belied her frail physique
"Come in," she said. "I know why you are here, and what you seek."
The woman, somewhat hesitant, walked in and looked around
Expecting more neglect, she was surprised at what she found.

The house was neat and clean and showed no hint of disrepair
The brightly painted walls conveyed an almost festive air
The appetizing smell of baking bread spread through the house
Evoking painful memories of times spent with her spouse.

The gypsy saw the welling tears the woman couldn't hide
Then took her hand once more and gently guided her inside
And when the gypsy looked at her with quiet sympathy
The woman let the grief and pain and rage she felt run free.

She spoke of how she'd loved her wife, how happy they had been
She spoke of devastating loss, of emptiness within
She spoke of shattered dreams, now dead and buried with her wife
And of the way she'd lost the joy she used to have in life.

She spoke of helpless anger at the court's corrupted ways
She spoke of bitter loneliness that filled her nights and days
She told the gypsy every single thing that had occurred
But of the reason she was there, she didn't say a word.

She spoke 'til day had turned to dusk and cast the house in gloom
But finally her voice trailed off and silence filled the room
The gypsy's face was grim as she considered what to say
"I know what you desire," she said, "and yes, there is a way."

"But heed me well, my child, before on this path you embark
The magic you would call upon is dangerous and dark
Think well on what you mean to do, look past your grief and pain
For that which you so wish for may not be what you obtain."

The gypsy, with dismay, saw that her warning was ignored
The woman's only thought was that her wife could be restored
Imagining her lover by her side alive and well
In avid haste she begged the gypsy for the magic spell.

The gypsy handed her a book, its cover black and red
"The knowledge you so keenly seek is written here," she said
The gypsy tried once more the eager woman's mind to sway
The woman mumbled vague assent and hastened on her way.

She hid the book inside her skirts and headed home once more
Ensuring all the shades were drawn, she bolted shut the door
Then started reading avidly, though not without some dread
For what the book described was how to resurrect the dead.

With simple illustrations and in words that seemed mundane
The book imparted comprehensive lore on rites arcane
The magic lured her with a promise she could not resist
Despite the voice inside her head that warned her to desist.

The woman studied carefully and planned how to proceed
She steeled herself to gather all the items she would need
A picture of her wife, some clothes, a lock of silken hair
She scoured the house to find them and collected them with care.

She read until she memorized the chants that she would sing
Repeating to herself so she would not forget a thing
Then purified herself in preparation for the deed
And waited for the dawn to come, for so the book decreed.

She set out in the early dawn, the town lay sleeping still
With head bent low, her collar up to ward against the chill
Toward the woods, between the trees she reached the river's bank
And finding a secluded spot, onto her knees she sank.

She dug without a pause, ignoring hands scraped red and raw
Until at last, to her relief, wet reddish clay she saw
Her slender body trembling with the cold, her visage pale
She gathered up the clay, unceasing in her grim travail.

Engrossed in her endeavor, with her clothes in disarray
Oblivious to everything she sculpted with the clay
Within her tortured soul a fierce determination surged
At length beneath her fevered hands a woman's form emerged.

She worked throughout the morning, driven on as though possessed
Her hands grew sore and blistered but she didn't stop to rest
With reverence she sculpted, every touch like a caress
Excitement coursing through her as she saw the work progress.

At last the task was finished, and her lover's shape was clear
She knew no hesitation though she felt a twinge of fear
She looked with love and yearning at the figure she had wrought
Then reached beside her for the bag of items she had brought.

Atop the figure's head she placed the silken strands of hair
And on the body scraps from clothes her dead wife used to wear
The picture of her wife she placed upon the figure's face
And prayed that soon a living form would be there in its place.

One final time she thought on the instructions in the book
Afraid that in her eagerness some step she'd overlook
At length she stood, her body stiff and aching, muscles sore
She knew her task was not yet done, the hardest yet in store.

On shaking legs she waded into water clear and cold
Her wooden pail she dipped and filled as much as it would hold
With heavy burden borne in arms grown weary from the strain
She struggled back toward the bank, her lips compressed in pain.

Forbidden words she uttered then, from secret, sacred chants
She circled seven times the clay, her mind set in a trance
While walking round she sprinkled water from the pail she held
Then all at once her heart with mingled hope and terror swelled.

The sculpture glowed a fiery red where water touched the clay
Thick clouds of steam rose up in waves from where the figure lay
Despite the fear she felt she never faltered in her task
Her features grim and pallid in a concentrated mask.

Another seven times she circled, sprinkling water still
Reciting different chants, her voice with fear gone somewhat shrill
But now where water fell upon the sculpture it transformed
Its features growing more pronounced as each spell was performed.

The reddish color faded to resemble that of skin
And fingernails and hair grew where before but clay had been
White teeth could only just be seen 'tween lips turned ruby red
And thick black lashes over rosy cheeks their shadows spread.

The woman watched the magic taking place before her eyes
So numb her battered senses barely registered surprise
Her one and only thought was that the end was almost near
Her lover would return to her if but she persevered.

The spell was almost done, the incantations all were said
The woman marshalled flagging strength, and then she forged ahead
She looked upon the form that bore the likeness of her wife
And spoke the word of power that would grant the figure life.

Long moments passed but all was still and silent, not a sound
In overwhelming grief the woman crumpled to the ground
With broken, anguished sobs she wept, her heart full of despair
When suddenly upon her skin she felt a breath of air.

Not daring to believe, convinced she must have lost her mind
She looked down at the sculpted form, afraid of what she'd find
When open eyes looked back at her, confusion in their gaze
She laughed out loud with joy, a sound she hadn't made in days.

She flung herself upon the form and held it to her tight
"You're back!" she cried, and felt the black despair she'd known take flight
With every passing second she could feel her sadness lift
She thanked the gypsy in her heart for giving her this gift.

Her hands were roaming everywhere, caressing every part
Relearning every cherished curve she held so dear to heart
She pulled the figure up with her and led it to the house
Content that she was once again with her beloved spouse.

That night, her arms around her wife, she slept a dreamless sleep
No sweat-drenched nightmares rousing her from slumber, sweet and deep
And when she woke with morning's light, her lover by her side
She felt complete, the way she hadn't since her wife had died.

And yet, not all was right, the woman couldn't help but note
Her wife was acting oddly, eyes opaque and face remote
Not speaking on her own, replying only when addressed
And even then with halting tones and simple words, at best.

The slender arms displayed uncanny strength not there before
Their movements were too slow and stiff to easily ignore
She tried to carry on, denying anything was wrong
But knew within her heart that she could not pretend for long.

She understood at last that which the gypsy'd warned her of
The magic had created but a semblance of her love
The soul could never be returned, for that there was no spell
The lover she'd brought back was no more than an empty shell.

And with that understanding white-hot rage engulfed her whole
The grief she'd briefly left behind welled up and filled her soul
Emotions swirled within her, too intense to be contained
Revenge and burning hate and anger, underlined with pain.

She cursed the men who'd brutalized and killed her wife in sport
She cursed the judge who, for his greed, kept justice from his court
She cursed the gypsy for the cryptic warnings and the book
She cursed her wife for not responding to her touch or look.

She stepped up to her wife and shook the passive form with force
"Come back to me! Come back!" she screamed, until her voice went hoarse
But empty eyes looked back at her, no answer in their stare
Until, at last, she turned away defeated, in despair.

Next morning found her walking on a path she'd walked before
Her fists were clenched with anger as she reached the wooden door
She knocked, then knocked again, but no one answered from within
And something eerie in the air raised goosebumps on her skin.

She pushed against the heavy door, which opened soundlessly
Then slowly stepped inside, and looked around her fearfully
The shock she felt was more than her beleaguered mind could take
Her last thought as she fainted was to hope she wouldn't wake.

The day outside had turned to dusk before the woman stirred
She moaned in pain, attempting to recall what had occurred
Then all at once the memories resurfaced in her mind
She stood and looked around again, but knew what she would find.

The once-clean house was full of dust, the floor obscured by grime
The painted walls were stained and yellowed with neglect and time
The gypsy's books and furniture were gone without a trace
And not a thing remained to show she'd once lived in that place.

And then, beneath the dirt, the woman saw a glint of red
She recognized the magic book and picked it up with dread
She turned the pages carefully and felt her eyes grow wide
For not a single word was written anywhere inside.

She let the book fall from her hand, and took one final look
Then walked outside and closed the door with hands that slightly shook
She headed back toward her house with heavy, dragging feet
Her head bowed low, her shoulders slumped, acknowledging defeat.

The woman understood at last that nothing could be done
She'd tried and failed; the monsters who had killed her wife had won.
But if she couldn't have her wife, at least she'd make them pay
And thinking of her lover's strength, she knew she had a way.

She set her lover to the bloody task that very night
The crescent moon was hidden in the clouds and shed no light
The woman followed after, treading softly and with care
But stopped cold in her tracks as screams of terror rent the air.

She crept up close until she saw her lover's silhouette
And came upon a gruesome sight she wouldn't soon forget
Upon the ground three men lay in a crumpled, bloody mess
The gory sight called forth a whimper she could not suppress.

For looking at the men the woman clearly saw their eyes
The shock and fear within too overwhelming to disguise
They cried and begged for mercy, but her wife did not relent
And beat them with inhuman strength until their lives were spent.

Her lover held a rod she must have picked up on the way
The men no longer screamed, their faces now a sickly grey
The sound of steel on human flesh came clearly from the fray
And rooted to the spot, the woman couldn't look away.

She glanced up at her lover's face and froze in disbelief
The once-blank eyes now clearly showed contempt mixed with relief
The pretty face was twisted in a savage, ugly grin
The woman reeled in horror as her blood ran cold within.

She knew beyond a doubt then that her lover was no more
And this was but a creature that her dead wife's likeness bore
Her sweet and gentle wife was dead, and never would return
She felt fresh grief like acid in her throat rise up and burn.

She ventured forward carefully, and touched the rigid form
Surprised, almost, when underneath her hand the skin was warm
The slender arms still held the rod, although the men were dead
And all around the ground was soaked in dreadful, garish red.

She took her lover's hand and pried the metal rod away
Then led them both from where the lifeless, battered bodies lay
She paused but once to look again upon her lover's face
But what expression she had seen was gone without a trace.

Through darkened streets, her wife in tow, she set a steady pace
With aching, heavy heart and bitter tears upon her face
And as she walked she hugged her lover to her, holding tight
The warmth against her side a source of comfort in her plight.

The journey seemed to last forever in her troubled state
But finally they reached the safety of their own front gate
She led her wife inside, and made quite sure she locked the door
And then prepared to let her lover go forevermore.

She washed her lover's hands and face and brushed the silky hair
Then stripped all clothing off, and laid her on the bed with care
She knew the time had come to bid her wife a last good-bye
She whispered tender words of love, but there was no reply.

One final kiss she pressed upon the lips she loved so well,
Once more caressed the rosy cheeks, and then performed the spell
A single word she uttered, hardly louder than a breath
Her wife's eyes fluttered closed, the muscles going slack in death.

The body slowly lost the likeness it had borne before
Becoming but a sculpted lump of clay, and nothing more
Returning to the river's bank she dug a shallow grave
And on a makeshift headstone set her wife's name to engrave.

The day was cool and sunny, hints of spring were in the air
The trees with tiny buds, and flowers blooming here and there
The woman never noticed, wrapped in misery and grief
Her only purpose now, in blessèd death to find relief

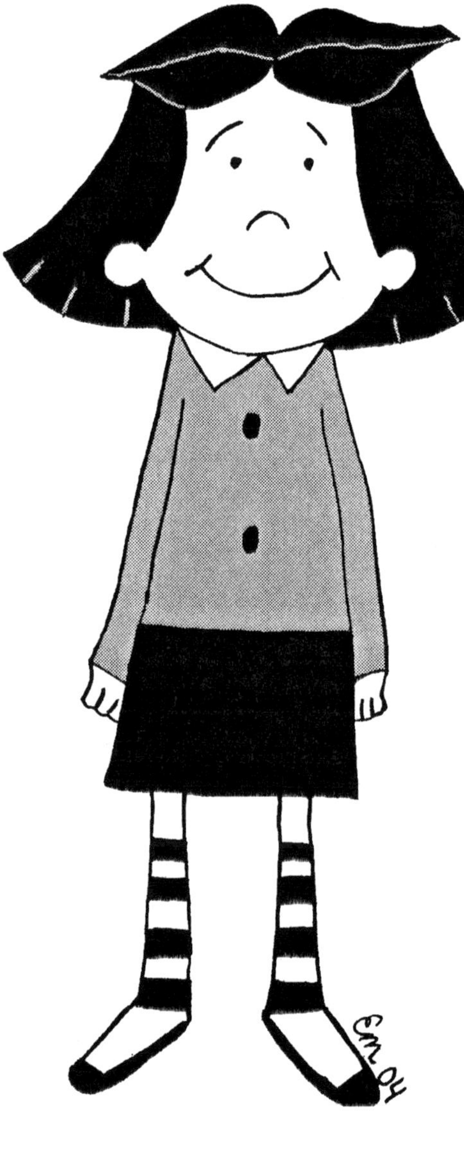
em 04

Author's Bio

Ms. Reed is a sometime physicist, sometime poet, whose role-model and inspiration is a famous inhabitant of Birdwell Island. Sadly, she has not been successful at acquiring a big red dog as a pet. She prides herself on her extensive wardrobe of knee-high socks and skirts.

Order These Great Books Directly From Limitless, Dare 2 Dream Publishing

Title	Price	Note
The Amazon Queen by L M Townsend	15.00	
Define Destiny by J M Dragon	15.00	The one that started it all…
Desert Hawk, revised by Katherine E. Standelll	16.00	Many new scenes
Golden Gate by Erin Jennifer Mar	16.00	
The Brass Ring by Mavis Applewater	16.00	HOT
Haunting Shadows by J M Dragon	17.00	
Spirit Harvest by Trish Shields	12.00	
PWP: Plot? What Plot? by Mavis Applewater	18.00	HOT
Journeys by Anne Azel	18.00	NEW
Memories Kill by S. B. Zarben	16.00	
Up The River, revised by Sam Ruskin	16.00	New scenes & more
	Total	

South Carolina residents add 5% sales tax.
Domestic shipping is $3.50 per book

Visit our website at: http://limitlessd2d.net

Please mail orders with credit card info, check or money order to:

**Limitless, Dare 2 Dream Publishing
100 Pin Oak Ct.
Lexington, SC 29073-7911**

Please make checks or money orders payable to **Limitless**.

I

Order More Great Books Directly From Limitless, Dare 2 Dream Publishing

Daughters of Artemis by L M Townsend	16.00	
Connecting Hearts by Val Brown and MJ Walker	16.00	
Mysti: Mistress of Dreams by Sam Ruskin	16.00	HOT
Family Connections by Val Brown & MJ Walker	16.00	Sequel to Connecting Hearts
Under the Fig Tree by Emily Reed	16.00	
The Amazon Nation by C. Osborne	15.00	Great for research
Poetry from the Featherbed by pinfeather	16.00	If you think you hate poetry, you haven't read this.
None So Blind, 3rd. Edition by LJ Maas	16.00	NEW
A Saving Solace by DS Bauden	17.00	NEW
Return of the Warrior by Katherine E. Standell	16.00	Sequel to Desert Hawk
Journey's End by LJ Maas	16.00	NEW
	Total	

South Carolina residents add 5% sales tax.
Domestic shipping is $3.50 per book
Please mail orders with credit card info, check or money order to:

**Limitless, Dare 2 Dream Publishing
100 Pin Oak Ct.
Lexington, SC 29073-7911**

Please make checks or money orders payable to **Limitless**.

Order These Great Books Directly From Limitless, Dare 2 Dream Publishing

Title	Price	Status
Queen's Lane by I. Christie	17.00	HOT
The Fifth Stage by Margaret A. Helms	15.00	
Caution: Under Construction by T J Vertigo	18.00	HOT-NEW
A Sacrifice for Friendship Revised Edition by DS Bauden	17.00	NEW
My Sister's Keeper by Mavis Applewater	17.00	HOT-NEW
In Pursuit of Dreams by J M Dragon	17.00	Destiny Book 3- NEW
The Fellowship by K Darblyne	17.00	
PWP: Plot? What Plot? Book II by Mavis Applewater	18.00	HOT-NEW
Encounters, Book I by Anne Azel	15.00	
Encounters, Book II by Anne Azel	15.00	
Hunter's Pursuit by Kim Baldwin	16.00	NEW
	Total	

South Carolina residents add 5% sales tax.
Domestic shipping is $3.50 per book

Visit our website at: http://limitlessd2d.net

Please mail orders with credit card info, check or money order to:

Limitless, Dare 2 Dream Publishing
100 Pin Oak Ct.
Lexington, SC 29073-7911

Please make checks or money orders payable to **Limitless**.

I

Order More Great Books Directly From Limitless, Dare 2 Dream Publishing

Title	Price	Note
Shattering Rainbows by L. Ocean	15.00	
Black's Magic by Val Brown and MJ Walker	17.00	
Spitfire by g. glass	16.00	NEW
Undeniable by K M	17.00	NEW
A Thousand Shades of Feeling by Carolyn McBride	15.00	
Omega's Folly by C. Osborne	12.00	
Considerable Appeal by K M	17.00	sequel to Undeniable- NEW
Nurturing Souls by DS Bauden	16.00	NEW
Superstition Shadows by KC West and Victoria Welsh	17.00	NEW
Encounters, Revised by Anne Azel	21.95	OneHuge Volume - NEW
For the Love of a Woman by S. Anne Gardner	16.00	NEW
Total		

South Carolina residents add 5% sales tax.
Domestic shipping is $3.50 per book
Please mail orders with credit card info, check or money order to:

**Limitless, Dare 2 Dream Publishing
100 Pin Oak Ct.
Lexington, SC 29073-7911**

Please make checks or money orders payable to **<u>Limitless</u>**.

Order These Great Books Directly From Limitless, Dare 2 Dream Publishing

Cat on the Couch by Cathy L. Parker	16.00	Hilarious
Kara: Lady Rogue by j. taylor Anderson	15.00	Adventure
The Amazon Nation by C. A. Osborne	15.00	Reference
A Woman's Ring by Rea Frey	16.00	NEW
Sweet Melody by Liana M. Scott	16.00	NEW
Deadly Rumors by Jeanne Foguth- OUT OF PRINT	15.00	VERY Limited
Walnut Hearts by Jackie Glover	17.00	NEW
Soldiers Now by Dean Krystek	16.00	November 2004
Home to Ohio by Deborah E. Warr	15.00	Mystery
The Mysterious Cave	12.00	Children's Adventure
Where Love is Not by Deborah E. Warr	16.00	NEW Ellen Richardson Mystery
		Total

South Carolina residents add 5% sales tax.
Domestic shipping is $3.50 per book

Visit our website at: http://limitlessd2d.net

Please mail orders with credit card info, check or money order to:

**Limitless, Dare 2 Dream Publishing
100 Pin Oak Ct.
Lexington, SC 29073-7911**

Please make checks or money orders payable to **Limitless**.

Printed in the United States
20612LVS00002B/82-144